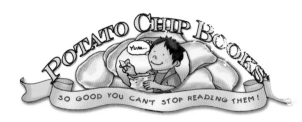

Up Here

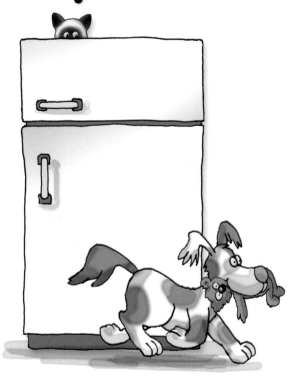

Written by Marilyn Pitt & Jane Hileman
Illustrated by John Bianchi

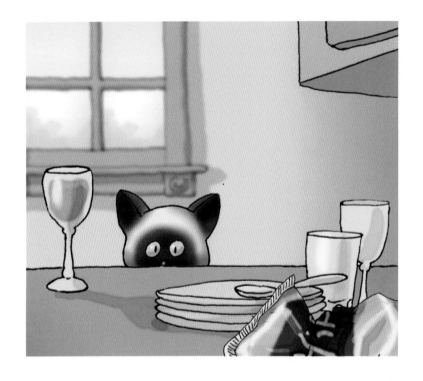

What is up here?

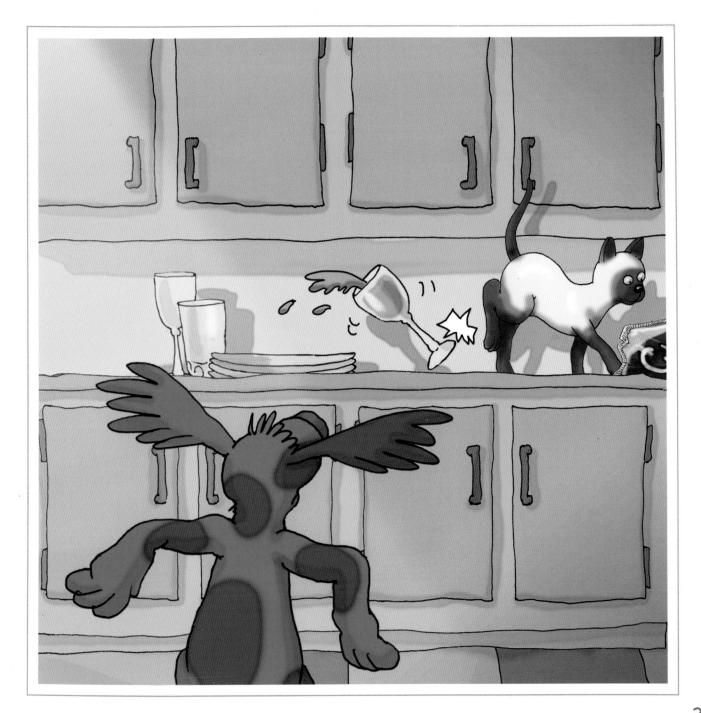

3

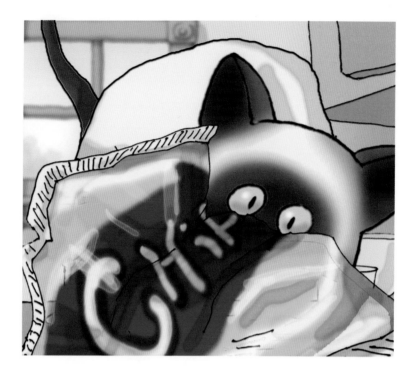

Is this for me?

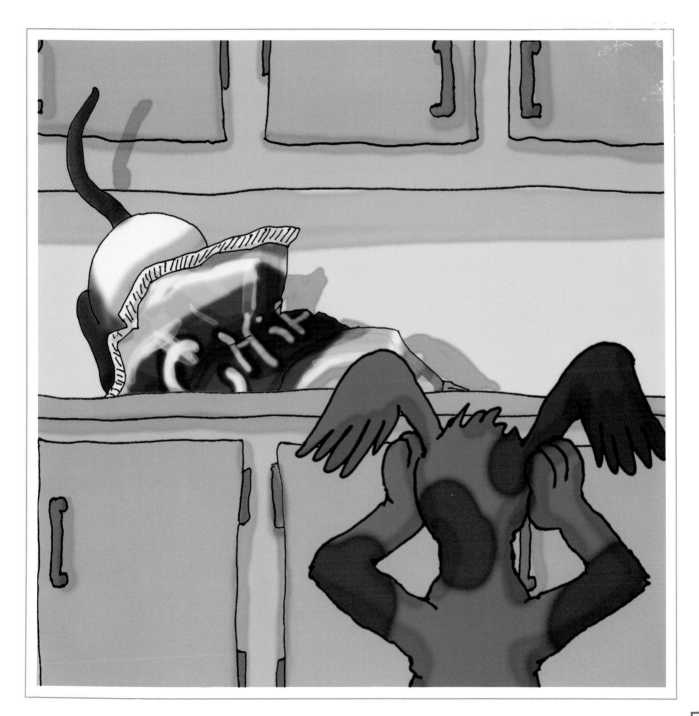

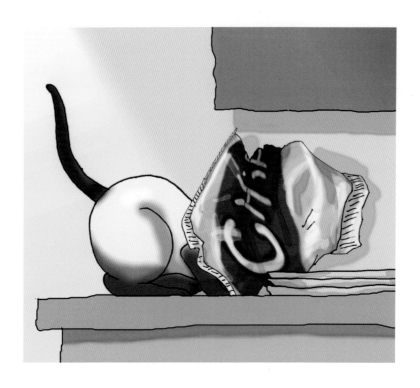

What is this?

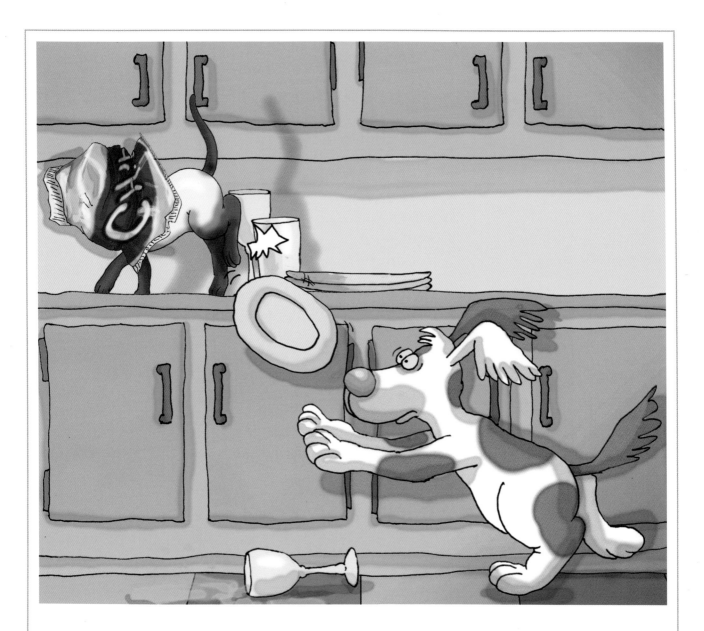

What is that?

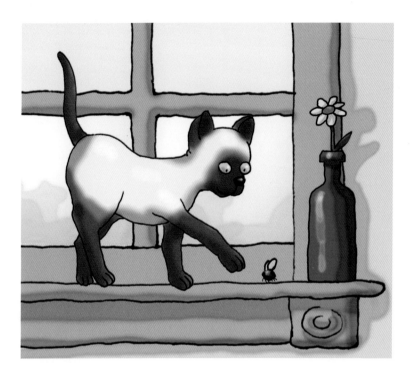

Is that for me?

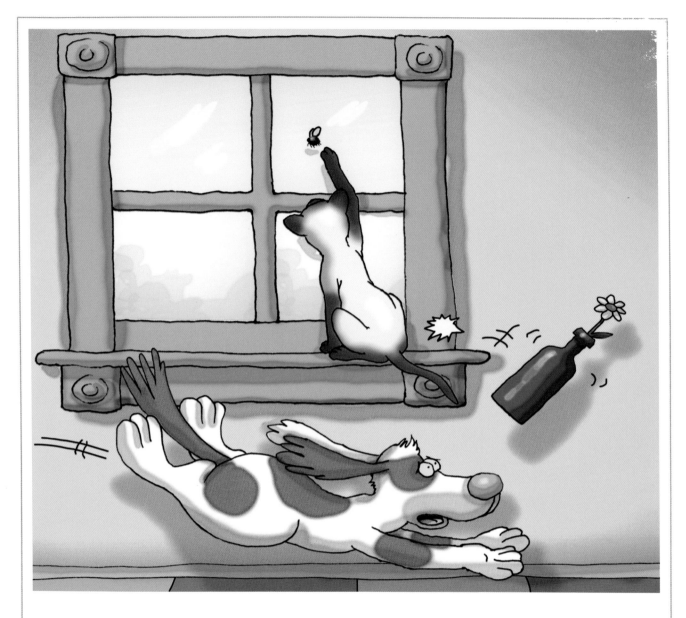

I like to get up here.

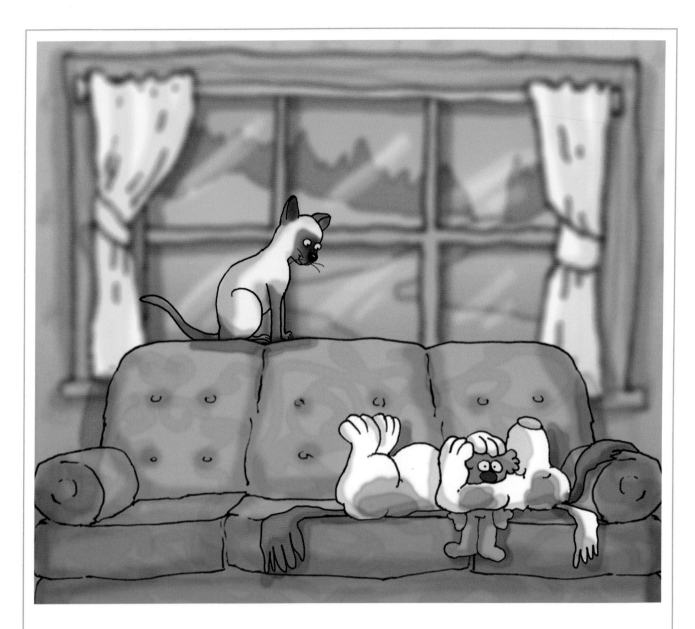

I like it up here.

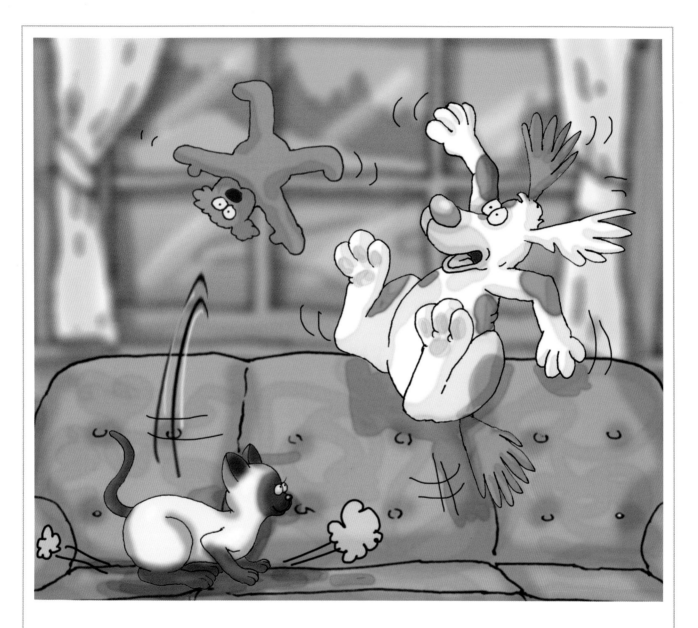

I will get down.

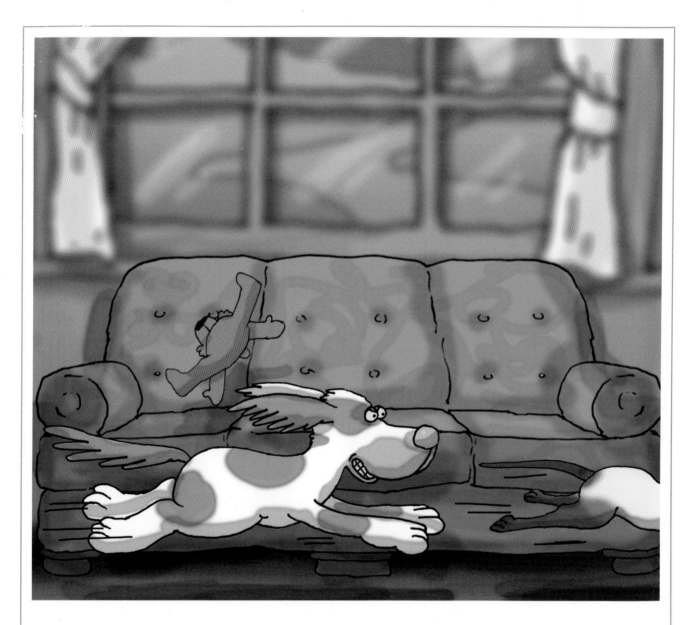

I will go!